welcome
little one

Welcome little _____

you were born on: _____

the time of day was:_____

your hair color was:_____

your eye color was: _____

your weight and length:_____

you were..._____

_____

_____

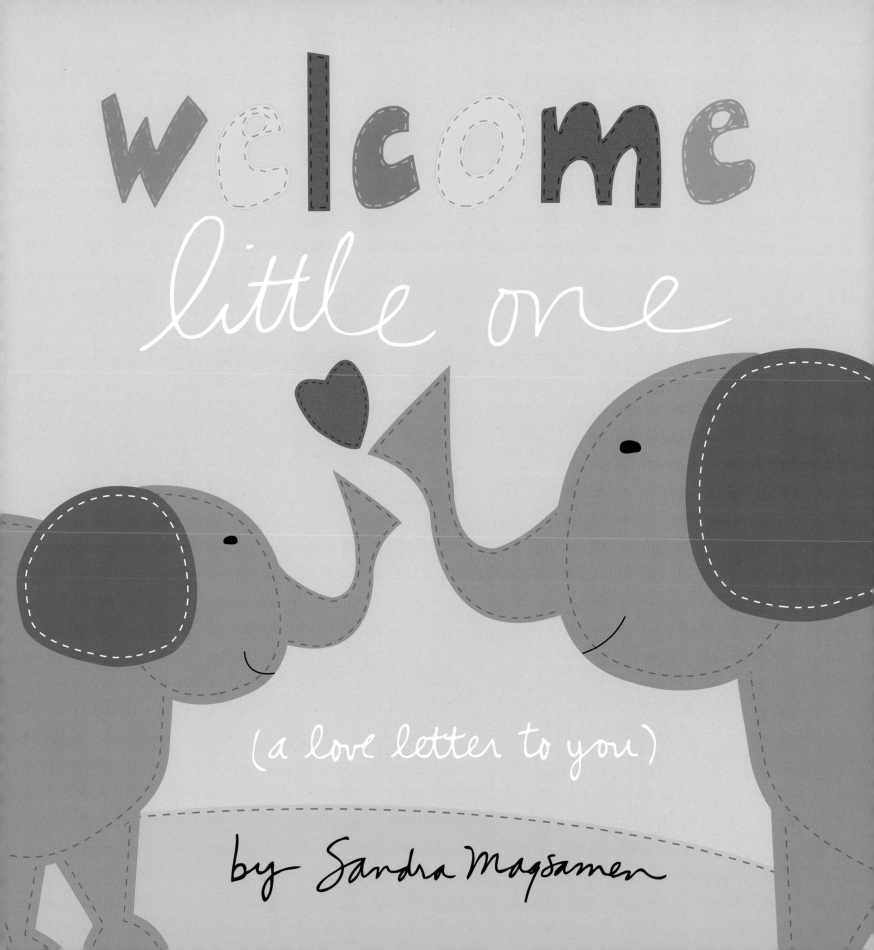

welcome
little one

(a love letter to you)

by Sandra Magsamen

On the day you were born, it was love at first sight. We welcomed you, little one, and held you so tight.

Our hearts simply grew bigger in size

the firs

looked

swee

ime we
nto your
yes.

Hope and happiness danced in the air.

Joy filled our hearts and spread everywhere.

We made a **Promise** to you
on that very day.
This, my precious
child, is
what we
had to say...

We'll **cherish** the things that are uniquely you— Your talents, your hopes, and your wishes, too.

We'll rock you to a song. We'
as you

..leep as we sing you
ead you stories
follow along.

We'll show you the
the stars i
Our love
with you
years

beauty of
the sky.
will be
as the
go by.

We'll teach you to see life from different points of view. And be there to help make your dreams come true.

The world became a more wonderful place, the moment we saw your beautiful face.

Published by Sourcebooks Jabberwocky, an imprint of Sourcebooks, Inc.
P.O. Box 4410, Naperville, Illinois 60567-4410
(630) 961-3900
Fax: (630) 961-2168
www.sourcebooks.com

Library of Congress Cataloging-in-Publication data is on file with publisher.

Source of Production: Leo Paper, Heshan City, Guangdong Province, China
Date of Production: February 2015
Run Number: 5002873
Printed and bound in China.
LEO 10 9 8 7 6 5 4 3 2 1

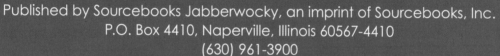